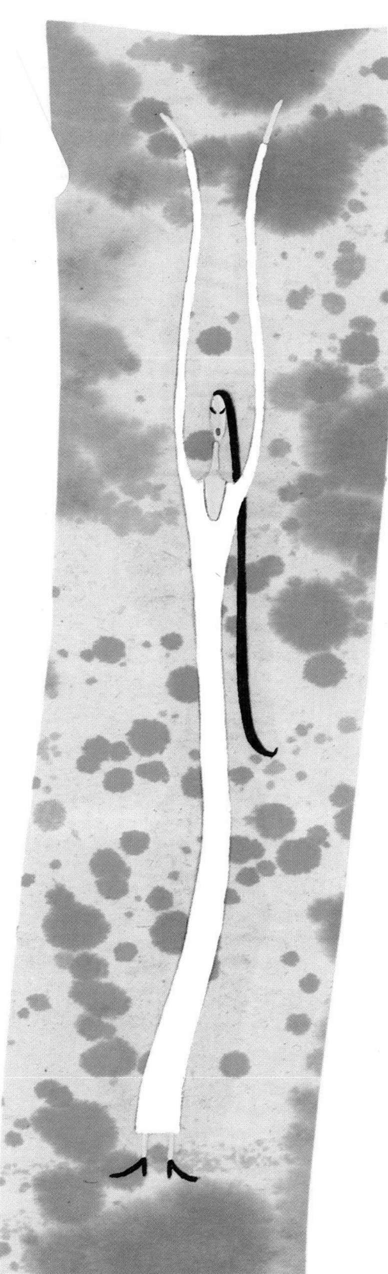

To Sam, Lorraine and Kaih,
and for Sue, for so much enthusiasm

Dots and Spots

First published in Great Britain by ABC, All Books for Children,
a division of The All Children's Company Ltd.

Typography by Francisca Galilea.
1 2 3 4 5 6 7 8 9 10
First American Edition, 1993

Library of Congress Cataloging-in-Publication Data
Morley, Carol.
Dots and spots / Carol Morley.
p. cm.
"Willa Perlman books."
Summary: A witch tries to steal all the spots from a town where everyone and everything is spotted.
ISBN 0-06-021526-7. — ISBN 0-06-021527-5 (lib. bdg.)
[1. Witches—Fiction.] I. Title.
PZ7.M82675Do 1993 92-24526
[E]—dc20 CIP
AC

Dots and Spots

Carol Morley

Willa Perlman Books
An Imprint of HarperCollins*Publishers*

Dotty lived in a spotty apartment in a spotted street above a fancy shop selling spotted hats and bags and shoes to fancy ladies in polka-dot dresses.

Dotty's
mother had
the very
important
job of
sewing
the spots
onto the
hats.

In fact, everything in the town was
covered with spots of all sizes and colors . . .

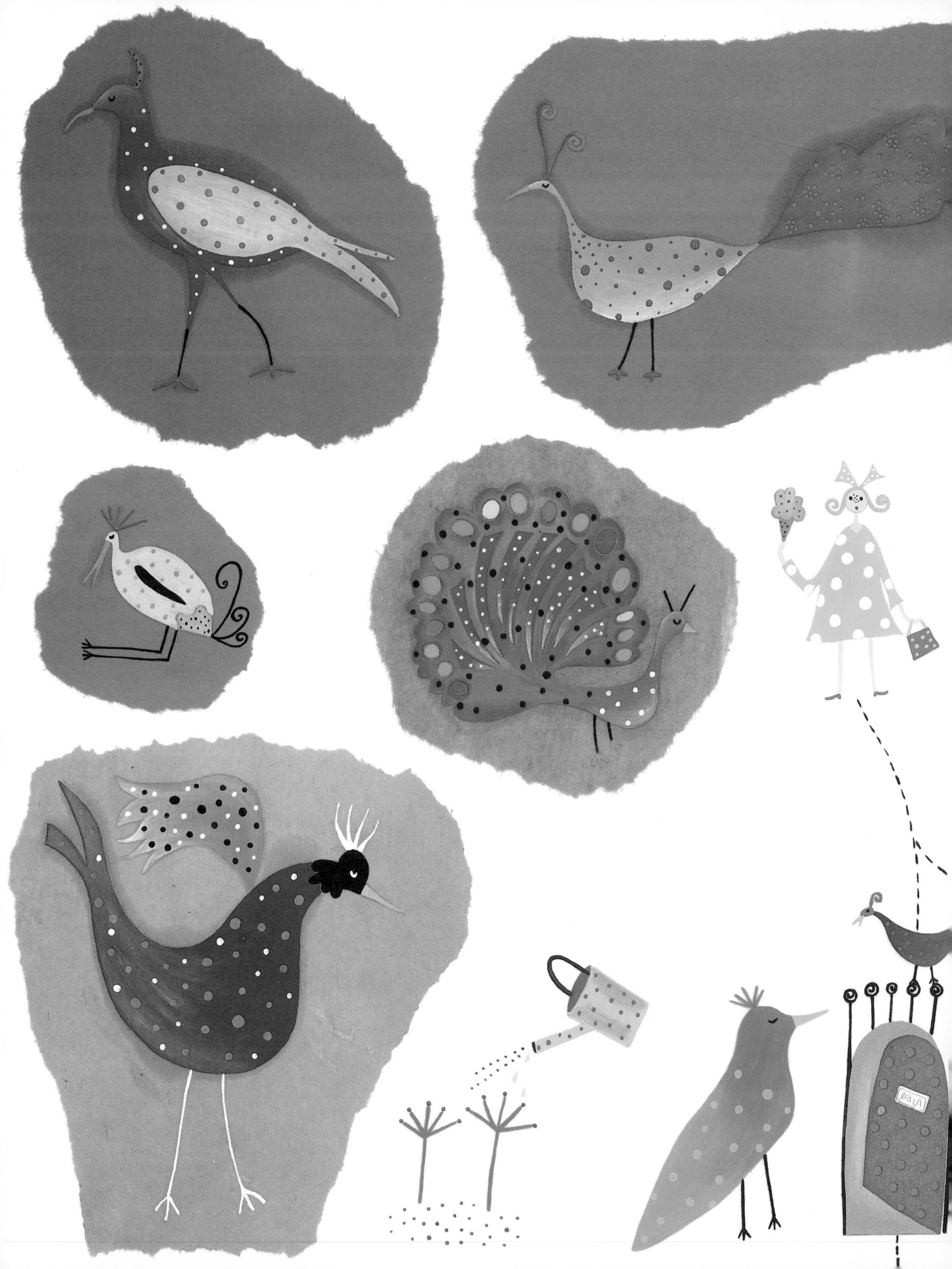

. . . animals, birds, flowers—even the people had freckled faces. Everyone in that town loved spots, and anything found dotless was usually given a quick sprinkle by the city's spot painter.

One night when Dotty was looking at the twinkling spots in the sky, she saw a strange car drive up and stop in the square. Out stepped a woman with long black hair and a *plain* white dress who looked up and down the street and then, with an evil smile, opened a hatch on top of her car.

I wonder what she wants in our town, thought Dotty as she got into her polka-dot bed.

The next morning Dotty awoke to moans and shrieks. From her window she saw the most horrible sight. Everywhere, dots dropped off dresses, spots spilled off spaniels, and freckles fell from faces. One by one, they swirled into the air and into the strange woman's car.

In despair and panic, the spotless
people ran after their beloved dots,

but they were whisked into
the air, and out of reach.

"So that's what that woman is—a wicked spot robber!" cried Dotty, watching in tears as her favorite polka dots slid off her dress and out the window.

Soon every dot, spot, and speckle was trapped, and the woman in white slammed the hatch shut.

"They are all mine now," she cackled, "and everything in sight will be white forever, just as I like it, unless you can break my spell. You each have one chance to guess my name, and if you can't, I shall snap my fingers and vanish from your spotless little town, never to return!"

The townspeople tried guessing names. "Spotlifter," "Blobburglar," "Dotsnatcher"; but none were right.

Dotty waited, staring at her favorite polka dots, trapped inside the car. They seemed to be trying to get her attention.

Suddenly, a smile appeared on Dotty's spotless face, and she stared harder at the car. At last, everyone but Dotty had guessed and failed. Then, in her loudest voice, she cried, "STELLA BLANGELLA!"

"Yikes!" screamed the witch
(for that was what she was).
"You've guessed! I'm finished!"

And, in the blink
of an eye, the hatch
burst open, and spots,
dots, freckles, blobs, and
speckles swarmed out
and flew back to their
proper places, where
they grew more
attached than ever.

Dotty was made Grand Chief Spot Keeper.

She never told anyone how she had guessed the witch's name. But she always took very good care of her polka-dot dress and wore it on only the very grandest occasions.

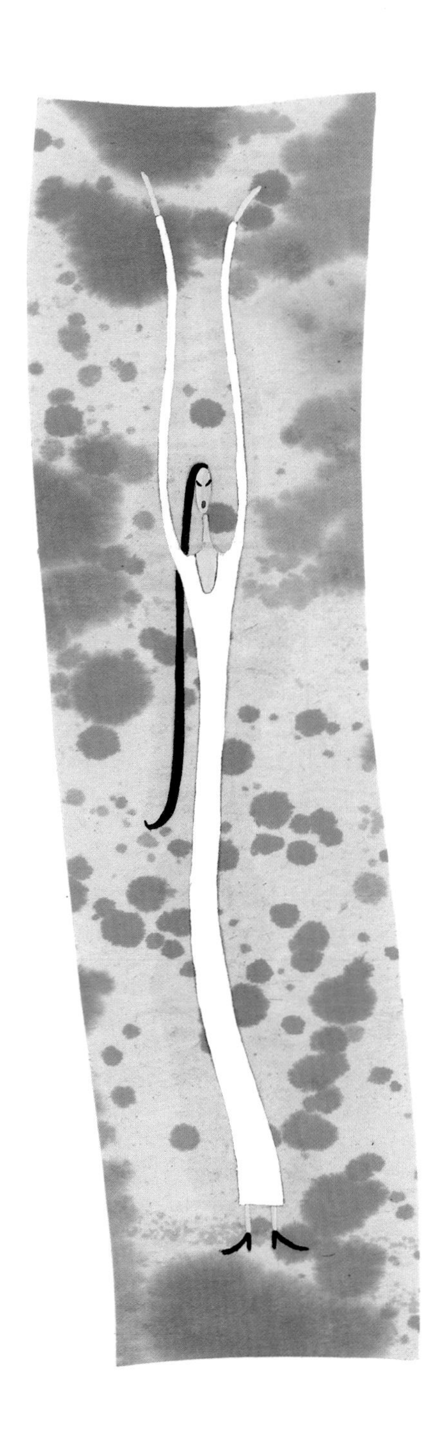